Edward T. Reed

Mr. Punch's Animal Land

Edward T. Reed

Mr. Punch's Animal Land

ISBN/EAN: 9783337238155

Printed in Europe, USA, Canada, Australia, Japan

Cover: Foto ©Andreas Hilbeck / pixelio.de

More available books at **www.hansebooks.com**

M^R P_{UNCH'S} "A_{NIMAL} L_{AND}"

"MR PUNCH'S" ANIMAL LAND

· DRAWN & WRITTEN BY ·

· E. T. REED. ·

· MAKER OF "PREHISTORIC PEEPS". ·

..

: BRADBURY, AGNEW & Cº. :
· LONDON ·

PREFISS.

There is two kinds of prefisses one if it is by
yourself and the other if you get a swell riter
to do it for you. I'm going to do it by myself because I have done the talk underneath the picktures so nice that I think people would be
greviously diseppointed if Mr. Andrew Lang or
somebody was to do it instead like he did for Sybil Corbetts book (thats the other little girl
what started "Animal Land"). He did it awfull
nice of course and then you can get such nice
things into it about your grate tallent and
your emaggynation if he does it. He is so lerned
and drags in illusions to other grate authers but
when you can auth as nice as what I can there
isnt really no need. If you do it yourself you
must appolergise for it all (they allways do) and
say it shall not accurr again. I am quite at
the openning of my corea (I saw that in the papers)
so I want ellowances made for my stile and imp-
erfect penship - I want it all put down to yewth.
    I have done all most all the most knowtable
Animals - you cant do everybody when youve got
musick and depportment to do too.
    (I never thought I would get to riting a Prefiss
but it is abserdly easey.)

P.S. I lernt to draw off the Veenus of Mealo and that
doesnt help you very much with these picktures. They
are mostly a diffrent stile of art alltogether.

Contents.

Contents.

The Hark

№ 1.

(Sir William Harcourt.)

Jugging by his exspresion I should
say he has just heard of some mill-
ionnares that is past recuvry.

The Hark

This Animal lives in a Resess in the Forest and
eats Orkids and Primroses. When there is
Krisisses and things about he chuckles. ——
He has a Party but it is mostly not there.

The Balph

№ 2.

(Mr. Arthur Balfour.)

Why. Ive left out his unkle who is
a moddle of peliteness to foriners.
He goes in for "Peace with — anything."

The Balph

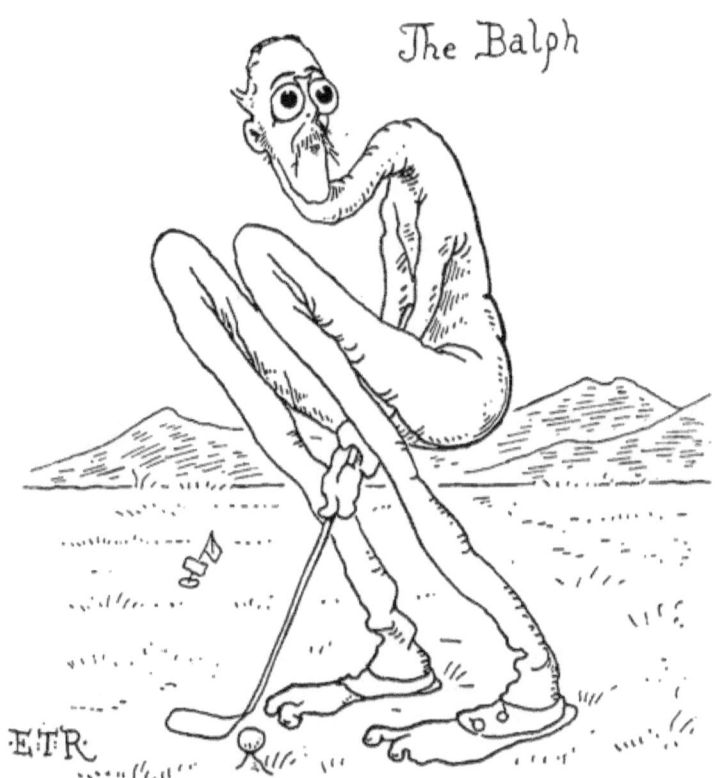

ETR

This fascinating Animal lives chiefly in a "bunker"
and feeds on stymies, cleeks, and voats of censure
it is very clever and has no ennemies but it
simply wont.

The Shuv

№ 3.

(Mr. Chamberlain.)

This is not a flattring likness but
there is a great fassination about its
rite eye if you look close

The Shuv

This Animal is a caution. It gets the best
of it. It likes to live in hot water and has
a nasty bite. It is better to go the other
way

The Oom

№ 4.

(President Kruger.)

I wonder why they say this is
"mannifessly inflewnced by
Landsere at his best".

The Oom

This strange old Animal is a wily one. He is very clever and disslikes strangers. Its not a bit of good to try to coax him he only says rude things and then prays and sings hymns. The Shuv has tried him all round but he only grunts and goes on praying

The Mailyphist
or
Gossplespredda

№ 5.

(Prince Henry of Prussia.)

The 'Kyow Chyow Vissitors List" says
"this is probbly a remarkable peece
of portritcher." It is all they ve seen
of him yet. His voice is certenly
somwhat prefracted.

The Mailyphist
or
Gossplespredda

This queer little animal lives on the sea as
there is not room for two of them in Germany
It crawls about trying to eet to China to fetch
some laurels and to plant shields and cathedrils
and things. If you have such a thing as a little
coal about you it will be very much obliged.
It will get there some day I seppose

The Pawkywit

№ 6.

(Lord Rosebery.)

I have been rather seccessfull in getting
the eger hopeful look into the gutesher
in his eyes haunt I

The Pawkywit

This dear little Animal likes to run
on the turf and that makes the good
ones start praying for him. It does not
like the Hark and has a dainty little way
of hiding itself among books and then it
waits and waits and waits ——

The Jook

No 7.

(Duke of Devonshire.)

The backround of this pickture is considered
by some to be my masterpeace. They say
it is just like a Corrow. I davesay it is.

The Jook

This Animal is very trustworthy but he is always fast asleep. He would much rather you did it if you dont mind.

The Benchiboss

No 8.

(Lord Halsbury.)

Oh! I forgot all about the Marquises -
they come first. That is an ovasite!
What a funny little dumpy he is!

The Benchiboss

This funny little Creature is very kind and never forgets a friend. He lives on a Woolsack and gives away things — — He has got a Earlship for been so good and clever so he comes next after the Joox.

The Labb

Nᵒ 9.

(Mr. Labouchere.)

I thought this would be baught for the
town-Hawl at northamter but some
malline influense must have been
at work

The Labb

This queer little Creature does not
like roads nor peers. It likes to get
into shady places and drag things out
into the light. If you pretend the Hess
is coming it will run into Wesminster
Abbey or anywhere

The Bujjit-Hatcha
or
Hicksybeech

№ 10.

(Sir M. Hicks-Beach.)

He does look a little bare and draughty. He would have looked better with his surplus on I think.

The Bujjit-Hatcha
or
Hicksybeech

This Animal is always trying to balance
things with a little over to one side. It
is very nice and plainspoken. It comes up
to every front-door just to see how you are
getting on and get a little something in the
pound? — It lives on beer and tobacco and
tin-tackses

The Wheedlepat

№ 11.

(Mr. Gerald Balfour.)

The criticks say this is "a life-like
pressenment" and the "flesh-tints
are remarkeble for there lewminos-
serty."

The Wheedlepat

This gracefull and culcherd Creature
has a very skillful way of getting on the
right side of people. They thought at first it
was a fish out of water but that was quite
wrong. It looks awfull solemm and poetick
but that is wrong too. It is very kind and
goes into every shanty and cracks jokes and
pats the pig. It has got a most bewtifull
bill coming which works like majick.
It lives on shammrocks and stetisticticks
with a few batons sometimes for rellish.

The Goash

№ 12.

(Mr. Goschen.)

You should hear his riddle about when a
lock-out is not a lock-out. It is screaming-
ly funny and evrybody has to give it up."

The Goash

This odd little salt-water Animal is very good
at sums and gets on pretty well with the
Esstimits. But if you ask him anything very
dificult he runs under the gallery to get the
answer. When strikes is on he is very kind
and doesnt expeck no ships finished — he looks
the other way

The Leck

No 13.

(Professor Lecky.)

It seems a grate risk for this one
to ventcher out into a rough
rude world. I wonder how he gets
over the crossings.

The Leck

E·T·R ♣

This gentle Creature is very   kind
and winsome so everybody likes it It has
a wonderfull brain and knows a lot.
When it sees a Artiss about it folds up
and tries to look like part of the Dado It is
almost a sin to make its picture

The Stagynite

№ 14.

(Sir Henry Irving.)

Some people consider this riting
very rude - it certeuly is not foolsome
in its prays.

The Stagyrite

This funny Creature gets up things very
nicely. When people go to see it it makes
the queerest noises and stamps on the floor
and drags itself about. I expect he
says it all right but you can't tell

The Ruddikipple

No 15.

(Mr. Rudyard Kipling.)

They say I have idellised him
rather but I cant help it if I
have.

The Ruddikipple

This little Animal is very strong and
vigorous and knows everything. If anybody tries to beat it it brings out a fresh
tail and then nobody cant touch that either.
It stirs everbody up so it would make a pew-opener
want to die for his country. If a Lorry it shews
his nose it just squashes him flat.

The Bobbz

№ 16.

(Lord Roberts.)

This is quite a battlepickture. The
handling seggests Mysonnyer.
I seem wonderfly versytial.

The Bobbz

This tiny little Animal is all pluck
and is full of beans, but he does not
try to spread himself like some do.
Directly an ennemy shews his nose he
has a neat little way of pulling it off.
All soldiers like him though he took
them very long walks sometimes. He
has got such a lot of meddles he has
to leave most of them in the cloakroom

The Showt

№ 17.

(Mr. John Burns.)

This is another full-face pickture. I
cant do many more of them!

The Showt

This little Animal is very honest and likes to fight. It has a very big voice on both sides – whichever it likes. It likes to get on a waggon in the Park and call out about wellth and capicklists and things. It sounds better out of doors

The Painticheef

No 18.

(Sir E. J. Poynter.)

I have heard he thought the droring of this very deaft and mastelly. I should have thaught it was a opper-tewnety for the Chantrey Fun but I have herd nothing as ⌒ yet.

The Painticheef.

This Animal is wonderfull clever and lerned
and plays at marbles with the Tadd. He stands
at the top of the stairs in among the plants and
goes on shaking hands with them all as they
come up untill he falls back exorsted. Then
they prop him up with ferns and collums and
things and he just bows till daylite. He has
got two awfull nice possitions to stand in too.
He keeps a warm comfitable home in Traffalger
Square for old worn out masters of schools that
are shut up. He is bredfull particular who he takes
in. He won't have them if they have gone cracked.
(I shall send this picture to the Acaddermy - he may
like to put it on the line in the Blacking-
White Room)

The Tass

№ 19.

(Mr. Alma Tadema.)

I cant help it if this did make mister Briton Rivvyare go green with envy. It must be ennoying to see an outsighder do it so nice.

The Tadd

This little Animal is awfull good at marbles.
Nobody cant do it like him. He knows all
about the ancients and what kind of boots
they wore on sundays and just how they use
to sit about and throw roses and make reff
lections on things in genneral. They did'nt
do much else acording to him. You can
allways tell where one of his picktures is
by the crowd of artisses round it - all putting
their noses ogenst it and then steping back
and striking silly atetudes. He has got such a
big voice that as fast as they stick the picktures up, it shakes them all down again

The Zolafite

№ 20.

(M. Emile Zola.)

This is diseppointing as a work of
Art

The Zolafite

This Animal is very bold and curvageous.
He is very clever at his work but he gets
very broad in places. The lower down thing
are the harder he tries to get them out.
The Troof is buried very deep Just now and
that is what he is looking for. So they are all
dancing with rage and say he is a Itallian

The Woolz

№ 21.

(Lord Wolseley.)

Sybil Corbett must be awfuly
mad to see me Sroring as good
as this. There is hardly a trase
of the ammerchewer.

The Woolz

This brilliant little Creature is a fearfull fiter
he is all over glory and titals and ilectrick-lights
He likes to have his battles ready overnight
then he does them in the erly morning before
the milkman calls when everyone else is in
bed and asleep. He gets all the powder and baynits
and cammerers and repporters ready and it can
all be in the papers the same day. Then he prases
everybody else for fiting so nobbly - it sounds
just like Warterlew - but some how there is not
so very many killed though it does look so terrible in
the lime-lite. That is his cleverness I expeckt.
Parlyment allways thanks him for it - he certanly
does make a neat job of it and he has such a nice
way of bringing home 'umbrellas and torture-chambers
and things to show he has really been there. If
he does anything else he will have to be made a
Jookdom.

The Klark

Nº 22.

(Sir Edward Clarke.)

This is a study in teckstchers and
keeraskewroh - and a speaking like-
ness as well

The Klark

This clever little Animal is a terror to fight. He covers himself up in silk and horsehair every day and then he runs along passages and pops into all sorts of diffrent cases one after another and draws a nice little screw out of them too. There isnt no need to be hanged while you can get him (I think this is nicer drawn than most of my picktures - I do hope he'll like it)

The Jappypote
or
Lytervaysha

№ 23.

(Sir E. Arnold.)

I hear he has a lovly _shrine_ to
write in at the Daily Tellegraff office
and the offise-boy burns joss-sticks at
him every harf hour. It helps him to
write nicer.

The Jappypote
or
Lytervaysha

This little Animal writes such nice
potery. He is found at all swarries with
his chest smotherd all over with stars
and krissanthenums and rising suns and
other ornaments. He has heard the East
a calling so he doesnt like London there
is not enough houris and dymios and
things about. They say he is growing
a pig-tail - he feels so orientle

The Reed

or

Bildaphleet

№ 24.

(Sir E. J. Reed.)

He says he did send his son to Harrow
what more could he do! Spelling must
have been an "extrer" I should think
It is a disstresing site to see the way
he does it.

The Reed   or   Bildaphleet

This splendid but desining Animal is awfull
good at shipps. He has a curious little taste
for liking them to keep on the surfiss and
flote the right way up which was very annoying
to the ammerchures who mannage these things
for us so nicely in parlyment. He is full of
stvength and boyancy and stellbility there
isnt no one quite like him I think — so is
his shipps they seem to last for ever as good
as new. He writes such vigorous letters that is
a moddle of viting and he is a good powelt to
It is a grate pity he didnt teach his son how
to spell he seems to get worse and worse — he
is a perfeckt <u>dissgrase</u>)

The Sullivan

№ 25.

(Sir Arthur Sullivan.)

I had the esistents of the leading
musickle exspurts in aranging
the musick on him

The Sullivan

E·T·R

This little Creature is full of the most
lovly tewnes and all other kinds of musick.
Nobody didnt know how humerous wind-ins-
trymants was till he did it. He will get a
trombown or a hoboy to talk just for all
the world like a rettired curnel only
funnier — it will make you ake with
laughing. He writes the most holy tewnes
too and makes you fancy you are soring
about with other angels in the upper-
boxes. (I wrote this wile goveness was out
of the room — she would say it was awfull
irevrent I exspect)

The Skippydan
or
Droorileno

№ 26.

(Mr. Dan Leno.)

I have had the nicest complements on this picture from Royal Ecademisians. They say it is so full of "vevve".

The Skippydan
or
Droorileno

This dear little Animal is never still for a
moment though it is full of wheezes. He is
very proud of his feet — you can see them if
you look carefully. Sculpters rave about him —
they say he is so stattuwesk

The Aird
or
Dammynile

№ 27.

(Mr. John Aird.)

The back·rownd seen of this picture
is laid at Filey-the-Beutifull where
the damms is to take place

The Aird or Dammynile

This kind Animal is allways so pleased to see you. He is very enterprising and has a funny way of contrackting himself and getting into the bed of a river and blocking it all up till it runs over. I should think the whole place will be full of crockerdials and irrigators and things. He has such a bewtifull beard - it looks as if he would make a very nice _prophet_, dont you think so

The Coneydoil
or
Shurlacombs

№ 28.

(Dr. Conan Doyle.)

This is a Alpyne seen. Please notise the way I have got the glare off the snow.

The Coneydoil
or
Shurlacombs

This big friendly Creature is very shrood
and saggacious. If he finds a footprint
he can tell you what colored hair it has
and whether it is a libbral or a con-
servetive - which is very clever I think.
He plays all games and always makes
a hundred. He likes to run through the
"Strand" with his tail in parts - all of
them strong and healthy - then he colects
it all together and it runs for a long time
by itself

The Timm

№ 20.

(Mr. Timothy Healy.)

I find profeels ever so much easier —
there is only one eye to rescle with
for one thing.

The Timm

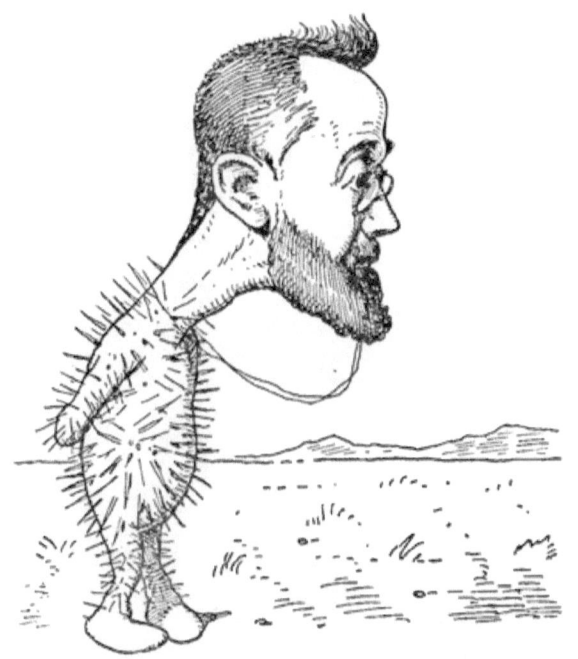

This prickly biting little Animal is about
the cleverest of them. He turns his back
round to the others so you can see he hasn't
got hardly any tail behind him. He has a
precius nasty sting though all the same that
will give you fits if you irretate him—it
will make you wish you were at some quiet
see-side place. He use to bellong to a party of
seventy but he has turned the other sixty-nine
out into the cold

The Leedabar
or
Dikkiwebbsta

№ 30.

(Sir Richard Webster.)

There is few drawings that has rowsed
more publlick inthewsiasum than
this one

The Leedabar or Dikkiwebbsta

This able Animal has such a noble
brain that there is only just room for it.
It cant get any higher without going right
out of the House. It sings like a bird and
says it fears no foe in shining armer but
hymms seems to suit it best I think.
Everbody likes it as long as it doesnt get
singing. It tried to make a apollergy
once but it was bredfully lame and couldnt
It lives on parchment and staind-glass.

The Trimmadome
or
Willirich

№ 31.

(Sir William Richmond.)

I _did_ enjoy doing his hair. It is
done like that Cleo de Merroads!

The Trimmadome
or
Willirich

This pleasant little Creature lives up inside a dome over a whispring gallery and
spends all his time sticking on nice little
pictures and patterns. You cant see much
of them from downstairs but he says
they are all quite religious and he is
very relliable

The Wagg
or
Tommibole

Nº 32.

(Mr. Gibson Bowles.)

Mr Spielman says "this remarkable
work is reddolent of the sea and
the droring of the wave-forms is worthy
of Hook or Eyrecrow."

The Wagg
or
Tommibole

This humorous little Creature is very
shy and modest. It lives on salt-water
and blue-books and what it doesnt know
isnt worth a dead star-fish. When ques-
tions is on it has a nice little way of
rubbing things in · It is always <u>there</u>

The Jingonite
or
Yankiturk

№ 33.

(Sir E. Ashmead Bartlett.)

Noboddy wasn't ever so pattriottic
about other peoples countries as
what he is

The Jingonite
or
Yankiturk

This odd little Animal did not grow
here you would think it had to hear it talk.
When it starts saving the Empier and
singing Rule Britannyer very loud they
only look at the ceiling and talk about
the weather and how long this is likely
to last

The Hyah-Hyah
or
Fisklekrank

№ 34.

(Sir C. Howard Vincent.)

He is a grate vollenteer too.
He is a mixtcher of Moltky and
Prince Ruepert at menoovers

The Hyah-Hyah
or
Fisklekrank

This popular Animal wants to know,
where everything comes from — then he
scribbles all over it. I believe it would
label its grandmother. If it can get anybody
to meddle with fiskle things it is quite happy
and cheers like winking. It has got a cheer
that is so loud that I expect it will be quite
out of order soon

The Kurnte
or
Armaghda

№ 35.

(Colonel Saunderson.)

I hear he has had this framed for
an air-loom.

The Kurnle or Armaghda

This pugonacious Animal is allways thirsting for slaurter. He has made himself such a nice dry ditch to die in if he can get the others to come on. He wears his coats all out dragging them along the flore so that somebody may step on them. If he can get anybody to stop and look he will eat fire like one o'clock - but it isn't real. Just at present he is taking the hat round. Everbody likes him tho, he is such a desspril charakter and so full of bloodtherstyniss. He draws nicely too - all exept swords - in fact he is quite a carickachuriss - like me, only I'm a perfeshernal

The Yauk
or
Rompyjack

No 36.

(Lord Charles Beresford.)

The criticks say I have "happily renderd
the sea-brease bloing through his
epithettes."

The Yauk
or
Rompyjack

This merry little Animal makes a good deal
of noise and never runs. He is quite at home
under fire or water. He just does it and that's
all

The Punchiboss
or
EphseeBee

№ 37.

(Mr. F. C. Burnand.)

This pickture and the nice ritin had
a wonderfull bennyfishle effeckt on
his state of helth

The Punchiboss
or
EphseeBee

This humrous little Creature has a most commical brain — full of happey thaughts. He settles on everything directly you put it in front of him. He is awfoll kind to chilldren so he gives me great enkuryoment when I do my picktures nice enough which is allmost allways now. He does buzz round you though and prod you up. He likes to get a good run on the boards sometimes. He has a skillful little way of knocking off a piece if it comes in his way — he is very strong in the wings. He has got a awfull clever lot of drawers and riters together — all of them genyusses and tipes of english beuty. (I must get this put in sometime when he is away — he might not like me to berlesk him after his polliteness and forcehight in letting me beggin so young.)

The Morl
or
Philopat

№ 38.

(Mr. John Morley.)

It is a shame to make such a nice gen-
tleman look so plain. There is no dowt
I am _not_ a flattrer.

The Morl
or
Philopat

This kind honnest Animal is very fond of dubblin and likes to play at billding a house on the green for them to fite in. He is wearing the green right throvgh with trying so hard. When he is on the steemer he nails things on to the mast. It is very odd he sits for Scotland and stands up for Ireland. He is a bewtifull talker and riter and goveness says he is a "pewriss in stile" (watever does she mean). He is struggling to learn the sord-dance over two vmbrellas. It is awfull hard thovgh and he keeps all on kicking his ankells till he has to sit down on the flore — then he plays on the bag-pipes like the heeros in India but the neybours do compldin so he will have to give it up or ellse move into another districkt.

The Fowla

№ 39.

(Sir H. H. Fowler.)

The "Maggasene of Art" thinks very highly
of this one – the "Morbydetser" of it is so
fine it says. I seppose they're right

The Fowla

This abill Animal is wonderfull strong and shrood and it can jump up and carry the whole house along with it if it likes to. It is very sollid and watey and has got a large dessenting body behind it. It knows all about howdahs and rajahs and things and it can turn pounds and shillings into roopees while you wait. It knows the diffrence bitween a millitry road and a footpath and if made it itself or if someone else did - which is more than some peeple do. It can make the forgiehammle wish he had never had a birthday. It is a very nice corteer and queens like it imensely. It wears a indian shorl on state occdjions, it doesnt fancy kilts. It is leeder of the libbral party - so is about half a dozen others too - they all do it at once but it dosnt matter much just now

The Kortnee

N° 40.

(Mr. Leonard Courtney.)

I wish the riting would not come so long but I'm ackwiring such preçishensy that I cant bring myself to shŏrt ones.

The Kortnee

This Animal has got a head full of rules and reggulatians. It is awfull fond of all kinds of riddles. the ones it likes best are those nobody cant make head or tail of - the abstuser the better. They make your hair all come off to think of them. He use to set in a chair and see they all behaved. He did it nicely that they mesured him for a bigger chair but it fitted someone else best so he lives in a tub now like Diodoiknees. He gives awfull nice lecktures to passers by and says order order to himself. He wants to have members of parlyment all difrent sizes according to the waight of the voaters - he calls it "prepporshnal repprisentatian" (I hope I have spellt it right) isnt it silly. He is a leedar of fashion. He has got a patent westcote of a very funny colour that is most becomming. They say he comes out all over brass buttens at night - he must look radiently bewtifull.

The Pass

No 41.

(M. Paderewski.)

Isnt it rather a sub-aubern tipe of face – not quite what you would exspeckt considdring the fuss.

The. Pass.

This curious little Creature never comes out
in the same place only about once a year -
that keeps his vallew up. They take him
round in a selloon carrige with his name
very large on the outside hermiticly seeld
and deckerated with maden-hare ferns and
rare browcades. They stop at the towns and let
him out to play for a few minutes then all the
ladies in sattly dvesses weep and gassp and shveek
out "Divvine! andsettra and rush about after him
till the pollice steps in - then they kiss the legs
of the piyanno and mone for a fortnight after.
　He looks more like a mopp than anything
I think.

The Thrums

№ 42.

(Mr. J. M. Barrie.)

I dont mean to say he doesnt bat very nice but he might just as well go for long drives out into the country.

The Thrums

This dellightful little Creature is very retiring
and knows a intervure diveckly by his stelthy
tredd. When he hears one he runs like litening
and gets under the sofer cushions or inside the
pexanno or crawls in under the slates till it is
all over. He use to live in a old licht-house once.
He is a marvelus mixture of the most conmical
humour and the most beutiful paythoss. He is
a regoular Ramsgitsingey at cricket. He
was to have gone to Orstralia with Mr Stodert
but they thought it was better for the Empire
that he should not. You should see him
snuck them among the slippers (I hope that
is right.) When he goes in to bat the fielders
all come close up to him just to take hints in
batting.

The Tobymp
or
Luciwits

No 43.

(Mr. H. W. Lucy.)

I had to leave the railings out or else
you wouldn't have seen him at
all

The Tobymp or Luciwits

This brilliant little Creature perches up
in a gallery and peeps through the ralings
and brings out the most wonderfull penny-
rating notes. He prettends to be asleep but
he is all the wide-awaker really. He has the
most lovely head of hair - they say it is some
kind of Essence what he has made up himself that makes it come so luxuryous. He
rubs it into the members too sometimes but
he has such a plessant skilful little way of
doing it all round and just touching on the
points of their bills that they rather like
it I believe

The Weeda

№ 44.

("Ouida.")

I had no idea I could do hair so
natcheral as this or I would have
done it before.

The
Weeda

This sentimentle little Animal is a most wonderfull disscriber - full of gaugeous colours. She has
a terrible fassinating kind of hero who goes out
to battle talking several langwages with a pardeent
-ya and lavinder kid gloves on and carrying a ormerlew
lunch-basket inlade with plovers eggs. He makes
little rings with cigerret smoke while he conkvers
the enemy. He is a mixture of Sandow and Cupid
and Bobby Spencer and Richard Curdyleong. She
is very kind hearted to other Animals. She was
thought rather risky for girls-schools sometime
ago untill all the Mrs Tankyrays started dragging
their "parsts" about - then it didn't matter

The Tree

№ 45.

(Mr. Beerbohm Tree.)

Isnt he nice and willowy. It takes a very clothes study of anattemy to draw pessitions like this.

The Tree

This pickturesk Creature moves about on
the boards in the most undewlating grace-
ful manner and likes to have a skillful
lime-lite man who can follow him about and
squirt it nicely all over his expreshun. He
has bilt himself a gorgeous theertre called her
magesty's because she dosnt never go near it
He is awfull good at maykupps. He likes to have
no end of collums all about him. The Tadd
has folded all his linen for him so nice that
he looks just like a real Roman figure. What
a washing-bill he must have with all those
toegers and forums and things.

The Lorryit

No 46.

(Mr. Alfred Austin.)

I meant to have drorn him trying
to get over a very rustick stile he's got
but I quite forgot. It dosn't matter
does it.

The Lorryit

ETR

This queer little Animal has got himself smotherd in with lorrels and he dosn't
hardly ever show -there has been too much
rime outside for him I expeckt . He is
allways hearing voices what nobody else can
Once it was like wimmen and children
screming out for help .Now it sounds like
Ammerican . It says it wants to have done
with its worn-out tail the tail of a anshent
wrong (It doesn't seem to mean much -does it)
When there is Royel babies going on he
has to sepply the Royel familly with nice
fresh odes and potery of a joyfull carecter
-That is what he is for - it must be a
dredfull life

The Ellen

Nº 47.

(Miss Ellen Terry.)

I am told miss Louie Freer is very much hurt at been passed over for this one but hers is a diffrent stile of luvliness - more like a <u>Wattow</u>.

The Ellen.

This gracefull and skittish little Animal is
a wonder to behold. She never seems to get no
older in spight of the lapps of time. When
she gets playing with the Stagynite the
congrigation go quite silly with rapcher and
they go on till they make her come out and bob
about and kiss her hands in the most commical
fashen. She is a wonderfull good Porsher and she
has got a very nice Oliviyer in stock too. As long
as she doesn't get too kittenish there is nobody
cant do it like her

The Sarabee

№ 48.

(Madame S. Bernhardt.)

This one seems to combine the suttle charm of a Rumney with the Seckvetive effeckt of a "peraffleite".

The Sarabee

This remarkable Animal is the idle of
the parizzians. It is very snakey and dra-
mattick. It has the most blood-kerdling
little ways of ettracting attenshen. When
it travles it takes black tiegers and coffins
and skellitens along with it to make peeple
talk and shudder. It has a most lovly ser-
ching voise that is ordible in the cheap
seats when you cant here a word the June
premyier has got to say for himself. It
is quite a sculpcher too in its way and has
got a stewrio where it paints in trowsers
That seems very forwerd and exentrick but
we musnt be too sensurious I seppose

The Villistanph

№ 49.

(Mr. Villiers Stanford.)

I havnt done justiss to the quire.
I havnt quite caught the look of agg-
ytashen and holy enthewsiasum in
there eyes — the mouths took up near-
ly all the room in the face.

The Villislanph

This tewnful and most versytial little Animal is hily skild at every sought of mewsick. He keeps a quirefull of mewsickle arristicrats that call obt Bach together. He persenally conduckts them through requiyumms and things and they get perple in the face trying to keep one eye on his conduckting-rod. It must be a great strane for the eyesite. He is awfull good at Irish jiggs too – that <u>must</u> be a plesant change for them all after the congrigashen is all left.

The Octavus

№ 50.

(Sir Henry Thompson.)

This is "a studdy of expreshen worthy of the best peeriads of english art" so the Stewdio" says "The impasse-toe is very fine" it says. I should never have thaught of that.

The   Octavus

This clever soshable Animle has got a
mainyer for eights of everything. Eight
gests - all sellybreighted - eight wines, eight
wayters, eight o'clock and then they all corrusc-
eight and sintilleight at him like anything.
He will soon be a octyoinnaryin all over — wont
that be a sellite to him. Hes a extrornary
surgen so he knows all about joints and things
and is wonderfull good at siyett. He spends all
his spare time tickling up the palette. He
is a grate bleever in creamashen and says
we shall come to it some day - I dont call that
pollite, do you. I thaught that was riserved
for those that is not regolar attenders at
church or made faces at goveness.

The Phil

No 51.

(Mr. Phil May.)

I exspeckt I shall have to pressent
this to the Nashnal Portret Gallry
- then I shall be handed down as
his " muniffisent dona ".

The
Phil

This commicle little creature drors
the hevenlyest picktures. He has made
the portrets of all the eyleet of Petti-
icote Lane. The critticks say he is a
"masster of teckneek". It must be very
nice to be called names like that — I
never get it. He drors a mixtcher of
Albut Dewra and Mr Sarjent and Sir
Danniel Leeno. He oans a most bewtifull fringe that few can rivle. I
didnt mean to give him sech a addul-
ating when I started — I do hope it wont
make him prowd and horty.

The Wunnubibbit

№ 52.

(The Perpetrator, E. J. R.)

I fear this will be a dredfull shock
to some but they say I musnt try-
fle with peaples effecktions any
longer. It seems a pitty to have to
rellinquish my "incoggnetow".

The Wunnudibbit

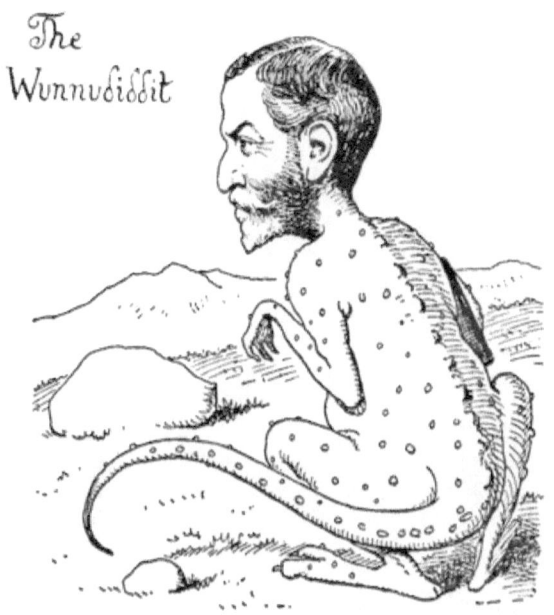

This abnoxious little Animal is the
anommylous auther of this Ceres. He
got all in among the Stone Age once and
kept all on doing the most elsurd picktures
He is a kind of Preestorick Pepys. They were
a ruff lot acording to him they ocupide all
there spare time chopping oneynother up
and dodging the most lothsome lumpy Animals. These picktures is coming out in
book-phorm now so this is the END.
What a releef to Crownd heads and others
that has got left out and what a mercy-
ful releese from his ettroshus stile of
spelling. How dredfull plain he is too.

·Tail·
-Piece·

www.ingramcontent.com/pod-product-compliance
Lightning Source LLC
Chambersburg PA
CBHW030133030726

47498CB00007B/2682